DISCARD

THAT'S GOOD!
THAT'S BAD!
IN WASHINGTON, DC

written by
Margery Cuyler

illustrated by
Michael Garland

Henry Holt and Company • New York

One day a little boy went on a class trip to Washington, DC.

When the kids got to Union Station, they climbed on board a DC Duck, *QUACK, QUACK!*

Oh, that's good!
No, that's bad.

The DC Duck drove past the White House. The little boy was so excited, he leaned out to get a better look, UH-OH! He lost his balance and fell onto the back of a motorcycle, VAROOM!

Oh, that's bad.
No, that's good.

The motorcycle roared to the National Zoo, where two orangutans were chasing each other across a high wire, TEE-HEE, TEE-HEE! The little boy thought they looked as if they were having fun.

Oh, that's good.

No, that's bad.

The orangutans scooped him up, WHOOSH! and tossed him back and forth until they got tired. They dropped the little boy into the back of a dump truck leaving the zoo, RATTLE-CLAP, RATTLE-CLAP.

Oh, that's bad.

No, that's good.

The dump truck bounced along to the Lincoln Memorial,
BUMPITY-BUMP. The little boy saw his class getting
out of a tour bus. The kids grabbed his hand and pulled
him up the steps to the statue of President Lincoln,
WOW!
HOW BIG!

Oh, that's good.
No, that's bad.

The little boy climbed down the steps,
but he didn't watch where he was going.
As he gazed out at the Washington
Monument, he S
              L
               I
                P
                 P
                  E
                   D

              and fell
            DOWN,
            DOWN,
            DOWN
          to the bottom,
          OUCHITY-
            OUCH!

Oh, that's bad.
No, that's good.

An ice cream vendor was parked by the reflecting pool.
He felt sorry for the little boy and gave him an ice
cream cone, SLURPITY-SLURP.

Oh, that's good.
No, that's bad.

REAL ITALIAN ICE

ICE CRE

No Ice Cream or Sod
in the Monument

It was a hot day, and the little boy's ice cream melted all over his hands, face, and shirt, YUCK!

Oh, that's bad.
No, that's good.

A parent helped the little boy clean up. Then they
got on the tour bus that was headed for
Arlington National Cemetery, HURRY UP!

Oh, that's good.
No, that's bad.

When the bus got to the cemetery, the class visited the Tomb of the Unknown Soldier. The little boy watched the guards marching back and forth in their shiny boots, TAP-CLAP, TAP-CLAP. He was so moved that he started to cry, SOB, SOB.

HERE RESTS IN
HONORED GLORY

AN AMERICAN

SOLDIER

KNOWN BUT TO GOD

Oh, that's bad.
No, that's good.

The little boy's teacher gave him a tissue. Then he led the class back to the bus. They drove to the Jefferson Memorial, RUMBLE, RUMBLE. The children got off and smelled the cherry blossoms by the Tidal Basin, SNIFF, SNIFF. The little boy thought they were beautiful.

Oh, that's good.
No, that's bad.

As they walked toward the steps of the memorial, a jogger ran by, POUND, POUND. He accidentally knocked over the little boy, OOPS. The little boy lost his balance and fell into the Tidal Basin, SLIPPITY-SPLASH!

Oh, that's bad.
No, that's good.

A man in a paddleboat fished the little boy out, DRIPPITY-DRIP.
He set the little boy in the back of the boat and paddled to the
dock, SWISH-SWASH, SWISH-SWASH.

Oh, that's good.

Yes, that IS good, because the class was waiting onshore. The teacher picked up the little boy and carried him to the bus. The little boy slept all the way home.

ZzZ-ZzZ-ZzZ.

WHAT A RELIEF!

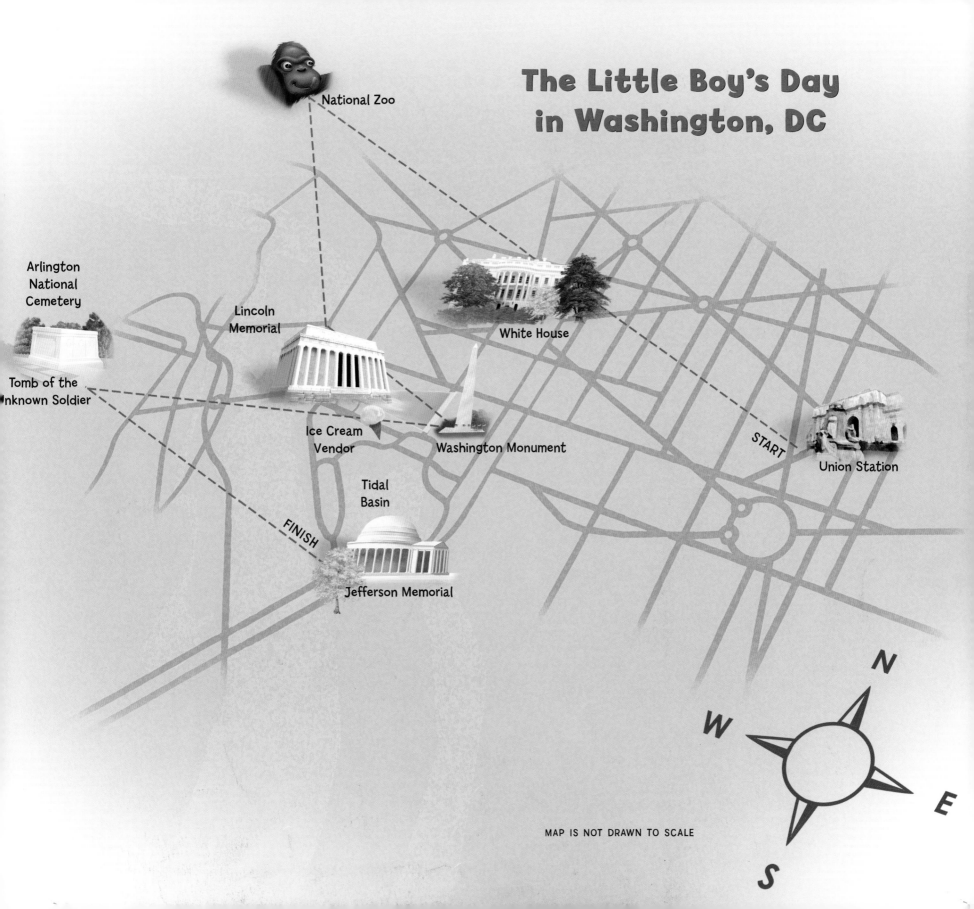

The Little Boy's Day in Washington, DC

National Zoo

Arlington National Cemetery

Tomb of the Unknown Soldier

Lincoln Memorial

White House

Ice Cream Vendor

Washington Monument

START

Union Station

Tidal Basin

FINISH

Jefferson Memorial

N
W
E
S

MAP IS NOT DRAWN TO SCALE

To Guy and Nancy McMichael

—M. C.

For my wife, Peggy

—M. G.

Henry Holt and Company, LLC
Publishers since 1866
175 Fifth Avenue
New York, New York 10010
www.henryholtchildrensbooks.com

Library of Congress Cataloging-in-Publication Data
Cuyler, Margery.
That's good! That's bad! In Washington, DC / Margery Cuyler; illustrated by Michael Garland.—1st ed.
p.   cm.
Summary: During a class trip to Washington, DC, a young boy has a series of mishaps, with both good and bad results,
as he and his friends visit the White House, the Lincoln Memorial, the National Zoo, and other landmarks.
ISBN-13: 978-0-8050-7727-8 / ISBN-10: 0-8050-7727-8
[1. School field trips—Fiction. 2. Washington (DC)—Description and travel—Fiction. 3. Tall tales.]
I. Garland, Michael, ill. II. Title. III. Title: That is good! That is bad! In Washington, D.C.
PZ7.C997Thd 2007   [E]—dc22   2006030764

First Edition—2007 / Designed by Amy Manzo Toth
Printed in China on acid-free paper. ∞

1 3 5 7 9 10 8 6 4 2

The artist created the illustrations for this book digitally.